Scary Stories

Gordon Armstrong passed away in the spring of 1996. He was a Vancouver playwright and described himself as a theatre school drop-out whose works include *Scary Stories, Blue Dragons, The Mona Lisa Toodle-oo,* and *Hashisch.* In 1992 he received a Sydney Risk Award for *A Map of the Senses. Scary Stories* was nominated for a Jessie Richardson Award. In addition to enduring eleven years as a theatre critic, he was a founding member and past-president of the Betty Lambert Society. At the time of his death he was working on two new plays, *Sex in Heaven* and *Curiousity.* His favourite horror movies included *Island of the Lost Souls* with Charles Laughton, Mario Bava's *Kill Baby Kill,* Fellini's short "Toby Dammit," and Georges Franju's *Les Yeux sans Visage.* His talent and energy will be missed.

SCARY STORIES

BY GORDON ARMSTRONG

Blizzard Publishing • Winnipeg

Scary Stories first published 1996 by
Blizzard Publishing Inc.
73 Furby Street, Winnipeg, Canada R3C 2A2
© 1996 Gordon Armstrong

Cover art and design by Robert Pasternak, with
technicolour assistance by R.K.W.

Printed in Canada by Friesens Printing Ltd.

Published with the assistance of
the Canada Council and the Manitoba Arts Council.

Caution

This play is fully protected under the copyright laws of Canada and all other countries of the Copyright Union and is subject to royalty. Except in the case of brief passages quoted in a review of this book, no part of this publication (including cover design) may be reproduced or transmitted in any form, by any means, electronic or mechanical, including recording and information storage and retrieval systems, without permission in writing from the publisher, or, in the case of photocopying or other reprographic copying, without a licence from Canadian Reprography Collective (CANCOPY).
  Rights to produce, in whole or part, by any group, amateur or professional, are retained by the authors.

Canadian Cataloguing in Publication Data

Armstrong, Gordon, 1960–1996
  Scary stories
  A play.
  ISBN 0-921368-63-1
  I.Title.
  PS8551,R7632S37 1996   C812'.54   C95-920255-2
  PR9199.3.A7763S37 1996

for Gregory and son

Scary Stories was first performed at the Martha Cohen Theatre in Calgary, Alberta, on February 3rd, 1995, with the following cast:

JULES	Hugo Dann
WALLY	Hardee T. Lineham
ELSA	Patricia Drake
ANGELA	Natascha Girgis
BLACK ANGEL	Shaun Smyth

Directed by Peter Hinton
Set design by John Dinning
Costume design by Carolyn Smith
Lighting design by Brian Pincott
Music by Allan Rae
Stage Manager: Bonnie Baynton

This production was co-produced by Alberta Theatre Projects and the New Play Centre. In March 1995, the production transferred to Performance Works in Vancouver, British Columbia, with Peter Beharry replacing Shaun Smyth as the Black Angel, and additional lighting design by Alan Brodie.

Introduction

Scary Stories is, on one level, a play about censorship. Which ideas and images are acceptable to society and which are dangerous? These issues became more explosive in any media that engages youth. In popular culture, this debate has been centred around film, television, rock music, and of course, comic books. What are we telling young people about our world? What are we revealing about ourselves? In the 1950s horror-sci-fi comics were held under scrutiny by an American Senate sub-commitee which deemed comic books to be dangerous beause they promoted juvenile delinquency. Comics relished in the strange, morbid fears and fascination of post-war America. Since juvenile delinquents read comic books it was resolved that comic books turned healthy young Americans to a life of crime and deviant behavior, sexual and/or otherwise. Dr. Wertham's book, referred to in the play, actually compares the threat of comic books on American youth to that of Hitler's Nazi Germany. In challenging comic books, the age of McCarthyism took on an enormously popular medium, and one which employed a prolific and brilliant group of writers and artists. Forty years later, we still contend with the effects of this challenge.

What responsibility has art to promote the values of society? How do we manage the expressions of our fears? Who decides?

While directing Gordon's play, I am continually struck by the authentic feeling of period he establishes in a recognizable modern voice. I think all really great plays do this. Using the fifties as psychological backdrop, *Scary Stories* tackles, in its metaphor, issues as contemporary as Eli Langer, political correctness, pornography, and the internet. Gordon selected a time in American history not to simply examine that place and time but, more importantly, to look at our own. If Gordon's metaphor was 1950s America for Canada today, that is a scary story indeed.

Every age has its own brand of horror and social control. In the fifties the monster was acceptable as long as its threat was perceived from without: aliens from outerspace; foreign vampires and zombies; monsters from the black lagoon. All these tales depict the terror of invasion and the ability to outface disaster by force, ingenuity, and the values of the heterosexual nuclear family. The stories which were censored, or perceived as dangerous, suggest that the monster really breeds from within. The horror may lie within our natures and the creature is the very system we have created to survive.

Liberated from the constricts and seriousness of high art, comic books were disposable icons of contemporary society and its attitudes to modern life, blurring lines between art and entertainment, social commentary and popular storytelling. What could be more potent than a medium designed to instill horror—all for ten cents an issue.

Importantly, comic books became good business. They thrived in the world of commerce, and moral decisions of appropriateness were also negotiated in the realm of profit and loss. In this context *Scary Stories* is indeed a play about the oppressions and censorship of the artist but also about compromise and the desire to be both critic and part of the system: Jules Chaykin is no Saint Joan and Wally Wolverton is no grand inquisitor. Jules wants his vision to unravel and upset but ultimately chooses the security and status of his position within the industry.

It is the tone of compromise, of facing enlightenment and choosing not to follow it, that provides the play's chilling conclusion. The characters all desire to expose the monster within but when faced with it roaring, they retreat and choose a path more conforming. However, once the monster has revealed its head, it is almost impossible to deny its existence. In the flash of an atomic bomb, the characters extol its beauty. This moment, like so many in this play, captures an aesthetic I knew in Gordon Armstrong. Gordon understood the comic potential of human treachery and the wickedness that often lies in the pursuit of the common good.

As a boy, Gordon loved comics and read them voraciously. As an adult he contined to indulge his passion for horror and fantasy in any medium from *Night of the Living Dead* to the stories of Angela Carter. All these references are present in *Scary Stories*.

Within all of us lies the monster and the censor. Personal conviction is neither a liability nor a refuge but each individual is left to negotiate his or her own struggle and either rise victorious or be vanquished. *Scary Stories* is a tragedy told with comic rhythms. It is a comedy with tragic implications. Its tone is something difficult to capture in production or imagine when reading. Each story told within the play is complete and satisfying unto itself. But each story also impacts the others, offering a shattering proferring of versions— of a truth hidden between Elsa, Wally, Angela and Jules. The apparent fragmentation between characters and the comic book adds up slowly piece by piece until the final bomb explodes.

In the end, *Scary Stories* is horror in the pure gothic tradition. Four people, alone in the house, in the dark on a stormy night, telling tales of horror and vengeance in which great and terrible secrets are revealed.

—Peter Hinton, 1996.

A Note on Casting

Scary Stories is a play for five actors, cast as follows:

The actor playing Jules Chaykin also plays BOLT, TROY and ROTWANG.

The actor playing WALLY WOLVERTON also plays AMBROSE, BILL and BARON OTTO VON ORLOK.

The actor playing ANGELA WOLVERTON also plays FLORA, MIDGE and SYBILLE.

The actor playing ELSA LOVECRAFT also plays CONNIE and ZAZA.

There are three incarnations of the BLACK ANGEL: a man on the piers; a masked and winged apparition; and as a synthesis of the prior two who appears in bondage during Jules's final monologue.

Act One

(Lights up on FLORA D'ARGENT, in showgirl-widow's blacks, talking on the telephone at a terrifically frou-frou vanity. The lighting is saturated with colour as in a comic book. Music plays: the second movement of Debussy' String Quartet in G minor.)

FLORA: What am I doing? Oh Bolt, don't tease me. I'm putting on my perfume, my Bénévole. You know I must! A splash from batch thirteen every evening, just as Ambrose stipulated in the mysterious codicil that his executor revealed only a moment before falling to the floor stone dead—if only that poison had worked faster! But I don't mind my Bénévole—after all, it is the last witch's brew, my last gift from the late, great perfumiere Ambrose D'Argent ... so kind and giving and stupid ... Besides, the perfume takes my mind off that smell, that horrible sticky-sweet scent of rot ... I seem to smell it everywhere now ... Even here in this room ... Bolt—oh, Bolt, I have the most terrible sense of dread! We've got to get away—I can't wait for the estate papers—we'll have enough to live on, we'll be happy, I promise. As long as we're free from Ambrose, that's all that—

(A noise, off stage.)

Bolt! There's someone in the house! No, I'm not—I can hear ... What if—what if he's not—what if Ambrose is still—Bolt? Bolt?

(She drops the telephone. Long pause.)

Who—who's there?

(Slow, scraping footsteps. FLORA produces a handgun from her garter.)

Who is it? I have a gun ...

16   Gordon Armstrong

AMBROSE: *(Off stage.)* Flora ... such a lovely scent you have on ...

FLORA: The smell ... the smell!

(AMBROSE enters, in an advanced state of decay.)

AMBROSE: I told you I'd love you forever, Flora ...

FLORA: Good lord!

AMBROSE: I told you I'd find you. My eyes have rotted out but I can still smell you, Flora ... I can smell your pretty perfume ... my gift to you ...

FLORA: No—

AMBROSE: How I long to kiss you, Flora ... No one loves you more than I do ...

FLORA: But—but you're dead!

AMBROSE: Not dead enough!

(The lights quickly come down as AMBROSE lunges at the screaming FLORA. BOLT appears, holding a car steering wheel, framed in a tight square of light.)

BOLT: What a chump I've been ... thinking Flora wouldn't blow her nut after we gave her hubby the long goodbye and thanks for the mazuma. If I can keep her from crackin' just long enough to collect on the jackpot ... Yeah, I'll take real good care of her—at least till she slips her gears on our honeymoon bicycle tour through the French Alps ... Heh heh heh ...

(The light on BOLT fades; the scene returns to FLORA at her vanity, her face hidden from view. BOLT bolts in, gun in hand, holding a handkerchief over his nose.)

Flora—what's this ungodly stench?

FLORA: Bolt ... I knew you'd come ... You're so good to me.

BOLT: Ugh—I'm going to be sick—

FLORA: He came back, Bolt ... Ambrose came back ... just for a kiss ...

BOLT: Flora—you've got to pull yourself together ...

FLORA: I think too many parts of me have already fallen off.

(She rises from the vanity and turns to BOLT. Her face is rotting.)

That smell, Bolt—it's *my* smell ...

BOLT: Good lord!

FLORA: Yes, Bolt, look at me! Ambrose always said his perfumes revealed the woman within ...

BOLT: No!

FLORA: ... and I've been rotting within for such a long time, my love ...

BOLT: Stay back!

(BOLT fires his gun; FLORA falls to the floor but instantly revives.)

FLORA: What's wrong, Bolt? Don't you want to kiss me ...

(BOLT shoots again, and again FLORA falls and revives.)

Don't you want to share my treasures?

(Her hands reach around his neck in a death-grip as she forces her mouth to his. Blackout. Two more shots. The music ends and JULES' voice, mimicking the "Dweller in the Tomb," is heard in the darkness.)

JULES: Yep, kiddies, seems poor ol' Flora pulled a real stinko when she asked for whom the smell tolls ... But why the grave look? It was such a scent-imental tale. Just ask any putrid perfume connisewer—when it comes to true love, the nose knows ... even when it's rotting off your face! Heh heh heh ...

(The scene is now the living room in the southeastern Nevada home of publisher Wally Wolverton. It is late autumn, 1954. The design is spare and elegant—a bar, a minimalist seating arrangement, very Frank Lloyd Wright. Upstage, there is an expanse of windows looking onto the desert and a slowly darkening sky, and a glass door leading to a patio.

WALLY is serving a drink to JULES CHAYKIN, who has with him a large art portfolio.)

WALLY: Great story. Creepy as worms, my friend. On the rocks.

JULES: Thanks.

WALLY: What a touch you've got. "The Benevolent Corpse." It's a classic, just like that one—the one with that living snapping skeleton creep aboard the ocean liner ...

JULES: "Bone Voyage."

WALLY: That's right—terrific story. Or that other one, the bloodsucker thing ...

JULES: "Scare Tonight, Followed by Increasing Clottiness."

WALLY: Right, right. Jeez, where do you dream up this stuff?

JULES: I live in lower Manhattan.

WALLY: Right.

JULES: So what do you think, Wally? The *Tomb of Doom*, issue twenty-one. Ready for the next lurid tale?

WALLY: Actually, I'm not sure I was ready for the first.

JULES: Come on, we've got some exceptional work here ...

WALLY: Sort of defeats the point of having a desert retreat, doesn't it, Julie? You flying all the way to Nevada to throw more work in my face.

JULES: You know why I—

WALLY: Oh, I know. I just don't believe it. What, did you spend your life-savings to do this?

JULES: Pretty near.

WALLY: Then you might as well take the time to enjoy yourself, breath the desert air.

JULES: Yeah, nice air, Wally. You should have it bottled.

WALLY: I like to share.

JULES: So do I. So on with the *Tomb of Doom* ...

WALLY: I'm not much in the mood for scary stories just now.

JULES: And never again?

WALLY: Look, Jules, I've shown you respect. My father taught me that publishing is a gentleman's business—

JULES: Your father published *Fuzzy Fables*.

WALLY: *Funny Fables*. Which I turned into *Captain Science* and doubled the sales, and then into *The Tomb of Doom* and sent the sales through the roof. And still stayed a gentleman.

JULES: Right, Wally, oozing with charm and dripping with blood.

WALLY: Look, I stood up for you—to a Senate subcommittee, for God's sake. I'm the one who had to sit in front of forty of the most brain-dead time-burners on Capitol Hill and explain to them why I publish comics like *Tomb of Doom* and *Weird Tales of Tomorrow*, why it was my top-selling artist who chose to depict a woman's skull split open and spilling its goo in a story about a crazy ax murderer.

JULES: The logic is obvious: you start with an ax murderer, you end up with—

WALLY: Face it, Jules—we're done for. Dr. Wertham's idiotic book saying delinquents read comics therefore comics create delinquents, it hits the media, then the goddamn Senate gets in it, now they want an industry censor—it's over. I'm killing the line.

JULES: Wally—

WALLY: I don't have a choice. The whole line—*Tomb of Doom*, *Weird Tales of Tomorrow*, *Crime Romance*—even *Zeena the Jungle Queen*.

JULES: Even the one you take with you to the bathroom?

WALLY: Seems Zeena got trussed up to a wooden pole by angry natives once too often.

JULES: Wally, you can't do this—

WALLY: You've read that damn code they're bringing in. Can't even use the word "weird" in the title of a comic—it's some damn foot-in-the-grave Methodist knitting circle wrote that crap. And it won't matter whether it's a bit of blood or a bit of bosom, without that precious seal of approval it's confetti fodder.

JULES: Man, you've got the best artists in the business. Look at Ingel's work for this issue—or Krigstein's stuff—it's brilliant ...

WALLY: It's too brilliant. That's the problem, Jules—we're trying to push an adult product in a children's market. When little Jimmy bounces home with a comic about a slimey corpse that strangles its two-timing widow, Mom and Dad aren't going to linger over the lush mood of the drawing or admire the nimble wit of the copy. We've got people screaming bloody hell out there—mothers' groups picketing news-stands; we've got people burning these comics—burning them.

JULES: So we give up.

WALLY: You think something like *Tomb of Doom* can fight back?

JULES: Yes.

WALLY: Look, Julie, I don't doubt you're disappointed. This is great work you've done, truly. And to think you were doing paste-up for Sears and Roebuck when I hired you. You know, I can only read your stuff when I'm in New York—never bring it back here with me. It's weird—I feel too creepy travelling with it there in my briefcase.

JULES: Afraid of getting caught with a trashy comic book?
WALLY: No, more like ... carrying a potent substance. A dangerous drug. And like any drug, Julie, you've got to stop some time. Here—let me top off your Johnny.
JULES: At least you're not shy with the good stuff when you can a guy.
WALLY: Oh, sure, you're canned from Fantastic Comics Incorporated, but Men's Adventure Publishing wants you so bad you're heating up the room.
JULES: Men's Adventure?
WALLY: Another thing my father taught me—one publishing firm, lots of names. Spread your assets around so if a title goes under, it doesn't take the whole inkworks with it. I'm pulling the plug on my comics line, not my business.
JULES: What are you offering me?
WALLY: See, now you're listening. I am offering you the best bone in the yard: glossy stock, full-colour reproduction, perfect ink holdout, any medium—airbrush, watercolour, you name it.
JULES: For a comic book?
WALLY: Not exactly. For a comic feature, in a magazine. Say, six pages, continuing character. Adult material, adult market.
JULES: What magazine?
WALLY: *Scallywag.*
JULES: A girlie rag?
WALLY: It's a men's magazine. I want a strip called Bouncin' Bonnie Bunny. It's satirical—she's a bunny but she's built like a babe. You have her bumble into these wild predicaments—make it as weird and funny as you want—monsters, mad scientists, J. Edgar Hoover—complete artistic freedom—isn't that what you're asking for? Just as long as Bonnie gets either tied up or undressed in each story—alternate it from issue to issue.
JULES: Tell me it's a joke, Wally.
WALLY: Top rates, Julie. No joke.
JULES: Why are you offering me this?
WALLY: You think I'd let you starve? With your fan mail?
JULES: And you think this is—appropriate?

WALLY: Oh. Okay—sorry. Not to your taste. Too ... robust, I guess.

JULES: It's a damn jiggle-toon! I'm sticking with what I'm good at.

WALLY: Julie, what you're good at isn't going to be around. I tell you, the whole industry, we're heading back to funny animals.

JULES: With breasts?

WALLY: If need be.

JULES: So the horror genre is dead.

WALLY: Drawn and quartered, Julie, a stake through the heart and its head on a platter. And this time there's no revenge of the corpse.

JULES: No, it's impossible. People are always looking for that—that *frisson*—

WALLY: That what?

JULES: *Frisson*. It's French. See, the French respect these things.

WALLY: Hell, Julie, even my breadsticks are from goddamn Wyoming.

JULES: *The Tomb of Doom*—it has history behind it—Petronius wrote a werewolf story in the Satyricon—and look at all the ghosts in Shakespeare—

WALLY: Yes, ghosts—not rotting corpses on a killing spree. It went too far, got too extreme.

JULES: So has the world. And these stories—they reflect that—the zeitgeist—

WALLY: Look, I don't speak bungo.

JULES: You know what I'm saying.

WALLY: Sure I know—I even think it's fascinating, this idea that it's a way to deal with all the terrible things that've ... I had the same talk with Williamson about all the mutant dinosaurs and the flesh-eating protoplasmic blobs in *Weird Tales of Tomorrow*—says it's A-bomb anxiety. So naturally—naturally I understand your devotion, this compulsion ...

JULES: Compulsion?

WALLY: Sure. Germany ... Auschwitz ... that stuff.

JULES: What?

WALLY: I figure you must had relatives or—I don't know ...

JULES: You gotta be joking. Wally, that stuff was a million miles away! I can't believe you'd think—
WALLY: How the hell am I supposed to know? I mean you don't ever mention your parents ...
JULES: There's nothing to mention. For God's sake, in their entire lives, my parents have barely set foot past the chachka palaces of Borough Park.
WALLY: But how could they avoid thinking about—
JULES: They're too sweetly bland to think about it—my god, my mother's so sweet she's raw on your teeth. Do you know how she liked to start the Sabbath? Every Friday, as soon as I got home from school, she'd make me burn my Supermans and my Green Lanterns in the fireplace.
WALLY: You call that sweet?
JULES: Oh, but she was, Wally—she's honey and nuts. The whole time, see, she'd be giving me this sweet smile, she'd be stroking my hair, like it was some wonderful favour she was doing me while I bawled my eyes out watching Superman shrivel to ash. Not that we talk about it now, let alone the war or anything—I swear if you mentioned the word holocaust to this woman she'd pass you another fruit pirishke and offer to turn down the thermostat.
WALLY: But—
JULES: Auschwitz is irrevelant.
WALLY: But surely not for ... all of you.
JULES: I speak for myself, that's it.
WALLY: Still, you get my point—And a kid's comic book isn't the place for—
JULES: So publish comics for adults.
WALLY: Right—like Bouncin' Bonnie—
JULES: No, like *Tomb of Doom*. Give me a glossy *Tomb of Doom* magazine, that's what I want.
WALLY: I'll lose my damn Fruit of the Loom! What adult is going to read that?
JULES: It's an adult product—you said it yourself.
WALLY: Yes, but—

JULES: What adult read Mary Shelley or Nathaniel Hawthorne or Edgar Allan Poe?

WALLY: Edgar Poe—he lived, he drank, he died, he gave the world severed heads stuffed up chimneys.

JULES: No, it was a whole body stuffed—

WALLY: What I'm getting at is this: things live, and they pass. People, comic books, ideas ...

JULES: No, not ideas.

WALLY: Oh, sure they do, all the time.

JULES: So we sit and watch them die?

WALLY: We move on. Okay, Bouncin' Bonnie Bunny isn't your style—I only asked 'cause you're the best. Why don't we try a super hero—as long as there's none of that Wonder Woman bondage stuff, and no lumpy he-man who takes showers in front of his boy sidekick.

JULES: I tried a super hero—remember? Doctor Thirteen, the nihilist magician. Didn't quite set our readership agog with awe.

ELSA: *(Off stage.)* Wally!

WALLY: Okay—a humour title.

JULES: You wouldn't appreciate what I find funny.

WALLY: A detective.

JULES: With no sex or violence? Snooze-ville.

WALLY: Then how about a pound of my flesh? What more can I offer you?

JULES: I told you—

WALLY: There's a limit! Trust me, Jules, you'll be better off if you'd just make terms with this.

ELSA: Wally!

JULES: I really thought you'd back me up, Wally. I thought you'd take a stand.

(ELSA enters, in a nurse's uniform with white pumps and silk stockings.)

ELSA: Okay, Wally—are you deaf or are you doped? *(Seeing JULES.)* Oh. *(To WALLY.)* Mrs. Wolverton is asking for you.

WALLY: I'm busy.

ELSA: Mr. Wolverton, you haven't seen your wife all day. She's wide awake.

(Pause.)

WALLY: Excuse me, Jules.

(WALLY exits; ELSA is already at the bar, mixing herself a drink.)

ELSA: So you're Chaykin.

JULES: Yes—well, Jules.

ELSA: How's your cocktail, Jules?

JULES: Fine, thanks. You're—you're not—

ELSA: But I am.

JULES: Oh.

ELSA: Mrs. Wolverton's private nurse. Elsa Lovecraft.

JULES: Really? That's not your real name.

ELSA: No, you're right, had it changed. Used to be Eleanor. *(Toasts:)* Chin-chin. *(She sings.)* "Have you heard, it's in the stars, next July we collide with Mars ..." Is something in the stars for Jules? Is that what brings you across the sand to Xanadu?

JULES: Trying to head off being terminated.

ELSA: And?

JULES: I've been terminated.

ELSA: That's nice. You can do something new. I love this view. The silent sky, that one lonely Joshua tree, and in the summer, purple grasses. And nothing else but distance. Did you drive?

JULES: Wally picked me up in Indian Springs. Flew into Vegas, then the bus ...

ELSA: I see. It's so far away here. Miles from anywhere. It's so far away, there's no one to hear you. In the night. In the dark. There's nothing between here and the town, and the town's as far as anyone will come in the night. In the dark.

JULES: What do you mean?

ELSA: I mean ... there's no one ... to hear.

JULES: Why do you say—hear what? What are you talking about?

ELSA: *(Laughs.)* I read it in a book. "In the night. In the dark." Just trying to get a rise out of you.

JULES: Shirley Jackson—"The Haunting of Hill House."
ELSA: Very good. See? I know all about you.
JULES: Me?
ELSA: You're the Dweller in the Tomb.
JULES: Well, sort of.
ELSA: I love it! And look at you—like you wouldn't raise your voice in a fire. I bet you have a secret torture chamber at home.
JULES: Well, a drawing board.
ELSA: I love it! Your stuff is so kinky.
JULES: You—you don't actually read the *Tomb of Doom*?
ELSA: Pornography of the nerves, I call it. Makes me tingle.
JULES: Wow.
ELSA: What's this? Oh—it's the original art! It's fabulous ... "Feeding William" ... I really mean it, your stories are wonderful.
JULES: Thanks.
ELSA: They really capture that feeling ... that dread of what comes next, but wanting it, wanting it to be ruthless, to throw open the doors of your fear. I want fear my whole body can feel.
JULES: Oh—wow—
ELSA: What?
JULES: Suddenly I feel like a hormone-injected lab rat at the Kinsey Institute.
ELSA: Is it that odd? I mean, I grew up being told stories about hungry trolls living under bridges and little girls who told lies and were burned to death. I suppose I do get a strange sort of comfort ...

(A vision of BILL appears; he is removing a blood-splattered surgical mask, gloves and gown.)

BILL: What bloody man is that?
ELSA: It's that feeling when suddenly the room gets darker.
BILL: Can you see me?
ELSA: The shadows change shape.
BILL: Do you know me?
ELSA: A face at the window.
BILL: I am eternal.

ELSA: A voice in the wind.

BILL: I am Banquo's ghost, shaking my gory locks, hissing, spitting, what bloody man is that?

ELSA: Sometimes it can just be the image—the eye at the peephole, the gleam of a knife.

BILL: The butchered phantom, I come at the last, called for or not.

ELSA: But sometimes ...

BILL: I come and with my kiss I cough my thick dark cloud ...

ELSA: It's more and it's worse ...

BILL: ... into the forbidden chambers of your heart.

ELSA: It's the idea itself ...

BILL: I am ...

ELSA: A twist of perception ...

BILL: I am but a thought.

ELSA: The aesthetic of pain.

BILL: ... a fearful thought ...

ELSA: The pervasion of disease.

BILL: ... which chills to the marrow with the fierceness of the delight of its horror.

(BILL disappears.)

ELSA: Loving the dead. Now there's a cheerful thought. You sure I can't top that off for you?

JULES: *(Unnerved.)* Thanks.

ELSA: But I suppose you know all that and more besides.

JULES: Actually, I think maybe you're too generous. I mean, it's just my way of looking at the world, that's all.

ELSA: Nothing's that simple.

JULES: No, really, I ... I like what the stories can say. But that's as deep as it goes—really.

ELSA: Hm. So if you're fired, will Wally still publish these?

JULES: He won't even look at them.

ELSA: Well, we'll change that.

JULES: Oh, well, thanks, but—

ELSA: I beg your pardon. I said I'll take care of it. You see, I provide certain therapeutic alternatives for Mr. Wolverton as well.

JULES: Oh.

ELSA: You twitched—I love that! Tension is so revealing. Here's your drinkie.

(Off stage, an abrupt shriek of unpleasant surprise is heard, then the sound of a slap and a crash.)

WALLY: *(Off stage.)* Ow!

(WALLY enters, teeth clenched, hiding his anger.)

I think she'd prefer to stay in her room.

ELSA: Too bad—Mr. Chaykin is about to show us one of his stories.

WALLY: This is a business meeting, Elsa.

ELSA: Not with this scotch it's not.

WALLY: Damn quick to recruit, aren't you, Jules?

JULES: Come on, Wally, I've got a fan here—a really, completely, undeniably adult fan. And she's dying to hear this.

ELSA: Dying.

WALLY: *(Muttering as he crosses to the bar.)* Damn damn damn ...

ELSA: This one, Jules. "Feeding William."

JULES: Yeah, you'll like this one, Wally—a simmering potage of psychological insight.

WALLY: Good clean fun.

(The scene begins to change as JULES speaks. Transition music: "The Work Song" by Charles Mingus.)

JULES: Well, my idea of fun. First panel: high-angle view of this nice suburban neighbourhood—see, very neat, houses lined up like a row of licorice all-sorts. Then, interior view: a model kitchen, beyond modern, right out of *Better Homes*. A young couple is eating breakfast ...

(The scene is now a terribly modern kitchen of the era, all glowing pinks and gleaming steel. BILL is having breakfast with his wife, CONNIE.)

BILL: Do the sausages four minutes each side—no more.

CONNIE: Yes, dear.

BILL: Broil the chops exactly six minutes each side.

CONNIE: They'll need twelve.

BILL: Six.

CONNIE: Yes, dear.

BILL: Sweetheart, you know you overdo everything. As for that liver—

CONNIE: I could simmer it in the Dutch oven, with little pearl onions and bacon bits—it would be so tender—

BILL: It's a five minute fry, Connie.

CONNIE: Yes, dear.

(BILL pushes his plate away. Menacing music plays, low.)

Bill—is there ... something wrong with your omelette?

BILL: I can't eat this.

CONNIE: But I whipped the eggs like you said—I didn't beat them ...

BILL: I've told my little kitchen angel what I like in an omelette, and it's not sauce.

CONNIE: But it's a Spanish omelette—

BILL: *(Pushing away his plate again.)* Well, a little nicely minced Spaniard is obviously too much to hope for.

CONNIE: Where are you going?

BILL: I have to get to the hospital.

CONNIE: You can't leave without breakfast.

BILL: Have a lovely day, dear. Don't forget your pills.

CONNIE: Bill—you can't—not without— *(She grabs a toaster from the counter.)* I'm warning you—I've got a toaster—

BILL: I think maybe someone has forgotten her little pills ...

CONNIE: The deluxe multi-slicer—

BILL: Here they are—

(She brings the toaster down on his head. Blackout. When the lights return, CONNIE has bound BILL to a chair. Food covers the counter, pots are simmering on the stove. Dizzy Gillespie's "Manteca" plays on the hi-fi, off stage.)

CONNIE: I do hear you, Bill. Creeping downstairs in the dead of night for that secret indulgence that's no secret at all—as if you expect me to know everything and nothing at the same time. We've had enough of these late night nibbles, William—I'm not letting you leave for work without a complete and nutritious breakfast. Honestly, sometimes I think you forget I ran that same hospital's entire nutrition department the whole time you were off saving soldiers' lives in the Philippines—and you think I'd be any less do-able here at home?

BILL: No, Connie—I don't—I don't think that—

(She feeds him from a bowl of hot mush.)

CONNIE: Of course you don't, dear. Dear William. Sweet William. Why else would you work so hard to buy me all these fabulous kitchen timesavers of tomorrow? Why, I'd be lost without my Zephyrion Mince-o-matic. Look—even inferior cuts like this low-grade pork shank come flowing out in a perfect cascade of shreds!

BILL: Connie—please—

CONNIE: And where would I be without my Mercury multi-speed Mighty Mixer with patented Qwik-whip—watch me puree this turnip in just seconds!

BILL: You've got to let me go ...

CONNIE: Oh, look, Bill, isn't it beautiful? I look at this and I think of ... well ... us.

BILL: Please, Connie—

CONNIE: *(Feeding him.)* Now, I know it's odd having puree of turnip on top of Cream of Wheat ...

BILL: Enough—

CONNIE: ... but a properly balanced breakfast shouldn't exclude an important food group.

BILL: Connie—I've got to get to the—to—

CONNIE: *(Feeds.)* The hospital.

BILL: Yes—I've got to—to—

CONNIE: *(Feeds.)* Perform surgery.

BILL: On—on a—

CONNIE: *(Feeds.)* Intestine?

BILL: Possibly.

(The sound of the oven buzzer.)

CONNIE: Oh! The confetti marshmallow pop-ups!

BILL: Connie—babycakes—please listen—

CONNIE: Yes, dear?
(Slight pause.)
BILL: Let's make love.
CONNIE: Bill!
BILL: We'll go upstairs and we'll—just untie me and we'll—
CONNIE: *(Emphatic.)* No, Bill. You haven't had breakfast.
BILL: Why are you doing this? If there's anything I've done to make you unhappy—
(She plugs his mouth with a pop-up.)
CONNIE: Isn't that yums? Oh ... I suppose I should put some newspapers down in case there's a mess, shouldn't I?
BILL: A mess?
CONNIE: No, I'll play it safe and throw down a tarp ...
BILL: Connie—
CONNIE: Here, Bill—you enjoy another pop-up while I run out to the garage ... and keep an eye on this pot of chicken a la king or your lunch will be—wait! What am I saying? It's the Avalon Autotemp burner-with-a-brain! No more pot-watching with carefree Avalon! I'm so lucky—I've got you and modern science! I'm the luckiest wife in the world!
BILL: What do you want? For God's sake, Connie—
CONNIE: Why, I only want to feed you, William.
(CONNIE exits. BILL throws back his head and moans. Then, desperately, he hops on the chair, trying to reach the door. A noise, off stage.)
TROY: *(Off stage.)* Dr. Flescher?
BILL: In here!
TROY: Dr. Flescher?
BILL: In the kitchen!
(TROY, a young intern, enters.)
TROY: Dr. Flescher! What's happened?
BILL: Just get me—
TROY: Who did this? Burglars? Commies? Koreans?
BILL: Troy—

TROY: This is terrible! Dirty pinkos infiltrating Miskatonic General! Torturing you for your lifesaving surgical techniques!

BILL: Shut up and untie me!

TROY: Oh! Sorry, Dr. Flescher!

BILL: That's Fleischer! Fleischer!

TROY: I'm sorry, doctor—I'm so darn jangled these days ... And when you weren't there to remove Mr. Osipov's uterine tumour—well, I didn't know what to do.

BILL: Find a knife—

TROY: Gee, I thought a scalpel would be—

BILL: For the ropes, not the stupid tumour!

TROY: Mr. Osipov doesn't think his tumour is stupid. He says it talks to him. Hey, is that a Jav-tone Flow-thru Miracle Filter coffeemaker you've got there? That's deluxe! I could sure go for a cup of joe ...

BILL: For God's sake, Troy ...

TROY: Sorry! Sorry, Dr. Flescher!

BILL: Fleischer!

TROY: Yes—sorry—oh God! It's this trouble I have staying focussed lately ... like there's all these different voices in my head. And the way Dr. Flem barks at me—man, he had me rattling like a milkshake-maker today. Dr. Flescher, you're a straight-talking fellow; let me ask you—do you think surgery is the right field for me? I mean, I wouldn't mind seeing somebody's inner workings—except they're always, you know, working, throbbing, pulsating ... man, it creeps me out.

BILL: The ropes!

TROY: Sorry, Dr. Flescher. Gee, I'm sure lousy with my hands. You know, a mouthful of hot java would sure—

BILL: There must be something—scissors—

TROY: Right! Not that I'm so hot with scissors either. It was really my old man who wanted me to be a sawbones like him. I think I'd do better in pediatrics—you know, helping society's young misfits ...

BILL: Yes, excellent idea ... Please, Troy—

(TROY starts making coffee.)

TROY: Dr. Flescher, I have something I want to confess to you ... I'm telling you this because I know you're someone who listens ...

BILL: I have no choice!

TROY: And that's a sign of your inner integrity. See, doc, it's like this: the whole reason I want to be a surgeon ... it's those outfits, the gowns ... They're so priestly. Like part of some holy ritual. When I was a kid, my big sister was a candy striper and, well ... something about her uniform, something so angelic ... I wanted to touch it, to feel the crisp pink cotton against my—say, this detachable Miracle Filter really is convenient!

BILL: Troy!

(CONNIE enters, carrying a tarp and a chainsaw.)

CONNIE: Well, I only hope you put gas in this chainsaw, Bill—why, hello Troy.

BILL: Damn—

TROY: Hi, Mrs. Flescher. Pruning?

CONNIE: A little work around the house. Helping yourself to coffee?

BILL: Look, can't you see what she's—

(CONNIE plugs BILL's mouth.)

CONNIE: Another pop-up, dear?

TROY: I'm sorry, Mrs. Flescher—I couldn't help—

CONNIE: Now, Troy, I can't have you fiddling about with my Miracle Filter.

BILL: She's trying to kill me—look—

CONNIE: Bill, really—Troy doesn't want to hear—

TROY: What is going on? Mrs. Flescher—I have to ask— you're not ...

CONNIE: Not what?

TROY: A fifth columnist?

CONNIE: Troy, what nonsense! Now, would you like me to fix you some nice hot coffee or not?

BILL: Look—look, Troy—the ropes, the food, the chainsaw—

(CONNIE silences him with another mouthful.)

TROY: Food ... chainsaw ... I don't know ...

CONNIE: All I'm doing is feeding my William.

BILL: To death! She's feeding me to—
(He is silenced by another mouthful.)
TROY: Mrs. Flescher!
CONNIE: Mugs are in that cupboard, Troy.
TROY: Oh—right. Look—I know it's real fruit loops to think you could possibly—
CONNIE: The Coffee-Mate's right there.
TROY: Thanks. But I gotta say, this doesn't look good.
CONNIE: It's not the worst thing this kitchen has seen. Tell me, Troy, do you have a girlfriend?
TROY: No.
CONNIE: A handsome, strapping lad like you?
TROY: I'm just sort of ... shy.
CONNIE: Goodness, I wish that was Bill's problem. He seems to take a consuming interest in every living thing.
TROY: And neglecting you, right? But that's only natural.
CONNIE: Oh?
TROY: Oh, sure, Mrs. Flescher—some guys, it's like they're nourished by every part of life. I see it in Dr. Flescher every day—in the operating theatre, or counselling patients, even when he's sweating it out on the squash court, damp t-shirt clinging to the contours of his back, perspiration marking a valley of muscle, his thighs gleaming like ... I'm sorry. I've said too much.
CONNIE: Not at all, Troy. It's natural that you should admire my William.
TROY: But are you really going to ...
CONNIE: Yes, Troy. I'm going to feed him right out of his skin. Mmm, tapioca ...
BILL: Oh god ...
TROY: But why?
CONNIE: He took my dreams from me.
TROY: From you, with this dream kitchen?
CONNIE: My linoleum mausoleum.
TROY: You could redecorate.
CONNIE: He's had affair after affair.

TROY: Well ... 'cause he's a guy.
CONNIE: He eats young boys.
TROY: What?
BILL: She's crazy, Troy—don't listen—
   (CONNIE produces a plate from the fridge.)
CONNIE: Whose heart is in the fridge, William?
TROY: Good lord!
BILL: It's a deer's heart—from my hunting trip!
TROY: Looks—looks human ... Good thing it's detached or I'd be out like the cat.
CONNIE: Bill, I want you to tell me whose heart this is.
BILL: You bitch!
CONNIE: Tell me.
BILL: I'll eat you too!
TROY: I think I—I think—
CONNIE: There's more coffee, Troy.
TROY: I—I've got to—
   (TROY goes to flee, but slips on the floor and falls, landing half-concealed behind the kitchen counter.)
CONNIE: Now look ... *(She sighs, then nudges TROY with her foot.)* Troy? Troy?
BILL: I heard his neck snap. It was almost a relief.
CONNIE: It's these episodes of perversion that drive us apart.
BILL: I gave you everything. Look at this home—I gave you this. Any woman would kill for what you have.
CONNIE: I am killing for what I have. Whose heart, William?
BILL: Freddy's.
CONNIE: Oh, Bill—a fourteen-year-old boy!
BILL: He was delicious. His thymus made an exquisite sweetbread.
CONNIE: You monster.
BILL: And you, my bride. And my cook and my whore. Don't tell me you've been ignorant of my appetites. Every morning it's been you who's primed me and set me loose on the world like a bubble in

the blood. Such love you've given me. If I'm the monster, you're my maker. And feeding me is all you're good for.

(CONNIE picks up the chainsaw.)

CONNIE: Then I won't stop now. Not when I'm just learning how to please your palate.

(She starts the chainsaw, lowers it over TROY. Blood spurts up; blackout.

When the lights come up again, the kitchen counter is covered with slabs of meat. A brain sits in the blender. BILL's mouth is stuffed with an unidentifiable portion of TROY. CONNIE is on the phone.)

And then bake at three-fifty for thirty minutes ... Tell me something, Trudy—can I use the spleen in this fabulous surprise 'n' kidney pie? Oh, wonderful. And the bladder—it's safe to freeze till truffle season? I see ... Oh, Trudy, what a wiz you are. I'm sure glad I know a hunter's wife—your George stalks those woods like my Bill stalks—what's that? Midge's boy? Why, no, I've seen neither hide nor hair of little Freddy. You don't say. True, you can't blame her. Listen, Trudy—gotta run. And thanks a million, okay? Bye-bye. *(She hangs up.)* Trudy is such a sweetheart. Her George is forever dragging home the most ungodly beasts—I finally understand why she never has time to help with our neighbourhood houseware parties. *(Checking the stove.)* The feet are boiling so nicely. Aren't you going to ask me what Trudy said about Midge?

BILL: Mmghff.

CONNIE: If Freddy's not home by suppertime tonight, she's calling the police. *(Sudden inspiration.)* We can have a backyard barbecue and invite them.

BILL: You're out of your mind.

CONNIE: *(Chopping and grinding.)* I've been out of it for quite some time—but you've been too busy snacking to notice, haven't you? This is my brain, William. *(She switches on the blender.)* A creamy puree, milk-fed and never put to use. Except to worry about whether I've made you happy. *(Feeding him.)* Have I? Have I made you eternally grateful for cul-de-sacs and busy kitchens, Galvano Eversharp, carefree Avalon and me, twinkling at the door in a polka-dot dress, a tall, cool Tom Collins in my hand, your slippers in my mouth and your throbbing ego-drill the one thing on my mind? You'd better be happy.

(A doorbell sounds.)

Ah, there's the grocery boy. I hope he remembered the paprika.

(She exits.)

BILL: My gut ...

MIDGE: *(Off stage.)* Connie?

(MIDGE enters.)

Connie, have you seen—good lord!

BILL: Midge—

MIDGE: Oh my—oh my—oh my—

BILL: Help me—Midge—

MIDGE: I'm going to be sick—

(MIDGE turns away. A sudden lighting change as she falls into a private reality.)

Where is my son? I'm looking for my son. We haven't seen him since last night—he ran out after supper, it was very strange, at first I thought he was just going out in the yard, but later I thought—the way he ran out, it was like he was eager, meeting someone, desperate to see someone. I've never felt that from him before. He's not even the age when I started to be afraid of boys—he's still a bit of a stick in his gym-strip, face still shines like a doll's. Is it starting younger, the wilderness that grows in boys? That sullenness. Like the child has finally found something to hate, something worth hating. Jim's out looking, driving around the parts of town we were so careful to never tell him about. Is he there? Does he know there's a dark, low path, a way to see the secrets in gaudy detail, and peel them away like leaves off an artichoke? The secrets of boys. I can't name them. I just want to find my son, so I'm looking—

(The scene returns to the kitchen.)

Bill—

BILL: Remember I told you—I told you Connie had become unstable ...

MIDGE: You mean she—

BILL: Get me out of here, Midge—before she comes back.

MIDGE: Oh Bill— *(She begins untying the rope.)* Does she know? Is that why?

BILL: No—not about us.

MIDGE: Are you sure? Oh, Bill, it kills me to think ... what we've done to her.

BILL: Don't think about it. We took what we wanted.

MIDGE: Yes.

(She goes to kiss him; he turns his head away.)

BILL: Not now, Midge—my wife is a maniac.

MIDGE: Oh. You don't want ...

(BILL rises free.)

BILL: You can't conceive of the things I want.

(CONNIE returns.)

CONNIE: Can you believe it—he forgot the pastry shells for the brain vol-au-vent—Midge!

MIDGE: Connie!

CONNIE: What have you done?

BILL: She's set things right. And oddly enough, sweetheart, I feel a bit of a wolf in my pit.

CONNIE: Midge—oh, Midge—

MIDGE: Stay back—

CONNIE: He's done a terrible thing—

BILL: Don't listen—

CONNIE: It's Freddy—

MIDGE: What?

CONNIE: He's eaten Freddy.

BILL: See? She's deranged.

CONNIE: He ate your son! And God knows who else. If you don't believe me, look in the fridge.

MIDGE: The fridge?

CONNIE: Look!

(Pause.)

BILL: Yes, go on, Midge. Look in the fridge.

(Low, scary music as MIDGE approaches the fridge and opens the door. BILL picks up an electric knife.)

MIDGE: What—what is it?

CONNIE: It's his heart.

BILL: Sorry, Midge. *(He switches on the knife.)* Promise me you won't go to pieces.

CONNIE: Bill, no—

(MIDGE starts to laugh.)

Midge—

BILL: What the hell are you laughing at?

CONNIE: Don't you understand? That's all that's left of your son!

MIDGE: My son was already dead.

BILL: What?

MIDGE: You see, I wanted him to always stay a boy, a sweet boy ... but I'd started to see a man in him. And I was frightened ... by what this man might do ...

BILL: What are you saying?

MIDGE: I poisoned him. Last night, at supper ... his macaroni and cheese was spiked with arsenic, nightshade and selenium; there was foxglove in his coleslaw, and monkshood in his spice-cake. And now it's all in you, William.

BILL: No—it can't be— *(He starts to choke.)*

MIDGE: He had to stay a boy, to stay innocent ... That's why I took that taxidermy workshop at the Miskatonic community centre ... It seemed the best way.

BILL: How could you—

MIDGE: It was ... When I mixed the arsenic into his macaroni ... it was a hard thing to do ...

BILL: You bitch ...

(He collapses.)

CONNIE: Bill!

BILL: I'll see you both in hell.

(He dies.)

MIDGE: Is he—?

CONNIE: Yes. He's dead. Oh, sweet William ...

MIDGE: Don't cry, Connie—don't—

CONNIE: He was the other half of me, Midge—the other half of my soul. *(She picks up the electric knife.)* And now—now you've destroyed that ...

MIDGE: He was the bad half, Connie—diseased—he didn't love you.

CONNIE: No, but he completed me.

MIDGE: Like I did once! Like I—can't you see—I had Bill because I couldn't have you—but now—please, Connie—please, why can't we start again? Why can't we love each other?

(Pause. CONNIE switches off the knife.)

CONNIE: Oh, Midge—

MIDGE: Connie—

(They embrace.)

CONNIE: Will you stay for dinner?

MIDGE: But Jim—he'll be home soon ...

CONNIE: That's fine—I'm sure we can whip up something tasty for him, too.

(Blackout. Music crescendos, then a gradual fade. JULES' voice in heard in the darkness.)

JULES: And this last panel—see? It's shaped like a valentine—like a heart—get it? A heart—and then our happy host-in-howls, the Dweller in the Tomb pokes out and says, "Well, boils and ghouls, how's that for grue love ..."

WALLY: Are you crazy?

(The lights come up once again on the living room.)

Eating boys, brains in a blender—that's psychological? And to have two women—to suggest—what do you think, Jules—you can have your cake, eat it, and throw it up in the face of Mr. and Mrs. America? This is exactly what we can't get away with anymore!

JULES: All the more reason to go for broke.

ELSA: I liked it. I thought it had bite.

WALLY: You know, you're starting to scare me, Jules—not your stories, you. You're a clever man, but—your zeal for this sort of thing—I mean, this story makes me feel like I've left some vital digestive organs back in my chair.

JULES: Because it made you confront—

WALLY: I confronted my scotch! There's some people you just can't scare—not this way—people who've got a grip.

JULES: A grip on a lie.

WALLY: And what's the truth—cannibals in suburbia? I think it's time you asked yourself why you like this stuff so much.

JULES: I like being scared.

WALLY: That's not an answer, Jules.

ANGELA: *(Off stage.)* Wally?

(Crash of a vase, off stage.)

ELSA: Damn.

(She exits.)

WALLY: Jules—look—let's not let this affect our friendship. It's strictly a business decision.

JULES: So that gives you permission to crap on me?

WALLY: I am not—

(ELSA re-enters, pushing ANGELA in a wheelchair.)

ANGELA: Is it time yet?

ELSA: She creamed your last Lalique, Wally.

ANGELA: Is it time for the big lights?

WALLY: Come and meet Jules, Angela.

ANGELA: Where are the big lights?

WALLY: Later. Angela, let me present Jules Chaykin. Jules, this is my wife.

JULES: I'm pleased to meet you ...

(He rises to greet her, but she simply stares back at him, not responding. He sits down again. She continues to stare at him, then places a porcelain doll on the arm of his chair and positions its head to direct its silent eyes at him. As the scene continues, ANGELA will surround JULES with an arrangement of dolls.)

WALLY: She's due for her medication, right?

ELSA: She's had all she's having today. But you can have some.

WALLY: Look at her—try—I don't know—one of the blue pills.

ELSA: She'll be—

WALLY: She'll be a lot easier to put back to bed.

(ELSA exits.)

ANGELA: I missed the big lights.

WALLY: The lights will be later. Just be patient, Angela.

ANGELA: We can play in the light.

WALLY: Well, not really, dear. *(To JULES.)* She means the A-bomb test.

JULES: The what?

WALLY: Tonight, over at Frenchman's Flat, in the big test site out there. Can't say I fault your sense of timing, Jules—you're in for the sight of your life.

JULES: We can actually see it?

WALLY: Hell, they can see it in Vegas. It's incredible, Jules—pure white, then yellow red, then flaming orange red ... an orgasmic dawn, the whole sky, twice as bright as day.

JULES: How—how do you know this? Does somebody just phone or—?

WALLY: Brochure in the mail. Here: "Our Friend the Atom."

ANGELA: Pink clouds. Pink.

JULES: Is it safe?

WALLY: Oh, sure, sure ...

ANGELA: And snow.

WALLY: Frenchman's Flat—that's a good fifteen miles—

JULES: Fifteen miles? Is that far enough away? Fifteen—

WALLY: Yes, it's safe, perfectly safe—look, it's all here. "Off-site warnings"—stay close to home and everything's fine—and this: "Radiation is nothing new."—There's radiation in our bodies, Jules! Natural radioactive carbon, potassium ... Believe me, it's safe and it's breathtaking. Chance of a lifetime.

ANGELA: Snow like cold smoke.

JULES: Okay.

WALLY: Good, you'll stay.

ANGELA: Burning snow.

JULES: Yeah ... yeah, maybe I have a story Mrs. Wolverton might enjoy ...

ANGELA: A story?

WALLY: Oh, sweet Jesus—

ANGELA: Tell me!

JULES: We've got time to kill, don't we?

WALLY: But not to slaughter, Jules. How much of this am I expected to take? And in my own damned home!

JULES: Look, I promise—no cannibals, no walking corpse, okay?

WALLY: I don't want to hear it. I don't want my wife to hear it. For god's sake, Jules, if you can't show some gratitude, show some consideration. I should be able to let you into my home without having to worry about—about—

JULES: Facing the fear that makes us—

WALLY: No, about the morality—about how long you can keep looking at sleaze before you become sleaze.

JULES: Ah! It finally comes out.

WALLY: Jules, I didn't say—

JULES: Oh yes you did. You think I'm sleaze. Funny—when I was making you money, I was your god-sent wiz-kid.

WALLY: You can be a wiz and still have some strange appetites, some unsavoury aspects to your life.

JULES: You don't know. I've been your damn slave—I don't even have time to loiter over physique magazines at the drugstore. Unsavoury? Unsavoury would be heaven. You don't know what it's like, shackled to my drawing board, four in the morning, helplessly staring out the window at the men slipping through the dark to the piers. You don't know—

WALLY: No, and I don't want to know, not about your brown-bag bars and your midnight walks and your—

(A sudden lighting change as JULES falls into a private moonlit reality.)

JULES: I could go. Go out. Just to walk. I don't have to go anywhere near the piers, I could just take the air for a block or two, look at the stars, look at the moon ... might help me sleep ...

(The BLACK ANGEL appears in its first incarnation as a dark figure of a man on the piers, lighting a cigarette and strolling solicitiously through JULES' reality.)

There's someone. Down on the corner. Pausing for traffic on a street without traffic.

No—come on, Jules—caffeine meets deadlines, sperm does not. Gotta finish this werewolf gig, this is the hairy beast I should be crawling inside, not ...

What if I did. What if I went. Just to listen from some secret place, listen to the explosions of hot breath, the soft moans as skin is shed, and the hair below bristles up with a crackle of static, and the body escapes the prison of the soul.

I know there's danger. I know people get hurt down there. Or worse. But that's ... isn't that part of it?

(The BLACK ANGEL disappears.)

What am I saying? I need some sleep, I need—No chance now of seeing even a sliver of morning, no fresh java, fleets of cabs, normal folk zipping off to normal jobs ... normal lives ... God, why do I envy the things I hate? Maybe—maybe the werewolf loves the silver bullet, he dreams of it boring through his wild heart, and the moon going out like the light draining from an eye. Or does he long to give himself over to an endless howl, a fierce, sad, helpless howl from the hot pit of his gut, claiming the darkness with a song of blood.

(The scene returns to the living room.)

WALLY: —or whether you stalk down young boys in Central Park— I don't know, I don't care—I just worry about a man who signs his work "Grisly." What kind of pseudonym is Grisly? I worry about—

JULES: You worry I'm sick.

WALLY: I didn't say that.

ANGELA: We're all waiting for dawn.

JULES: Grisly the psycho homo Jew—that's how you see me?

WALLY: Jules, don't say those things!

ANGELA: Quiet in the dark ...

WALLY: It's asking for trouble.

JULES: From who—the Comics Code Authority? I'm shaking!

ANGELA: Quiet, quiet ...

JULES: What do you think, Wally—I'm the disease? I'm the love of death, standing right here in your own living room?

WALLY: Jules—

JULES: My god, I'm the pathology that creeps by night! That's psychological?

(ANGELA flings a doll away from her.)

ANGELA: Don't look at me like that!

WALLY: Now, see what you've—

JULES: Let me have my say, damn it!

ANGELA: The blue eyes of the broken doll ...

(ELSA enters with a hypodermic needle.)

ELSA: Wally ...

WALLY: I need another scotch ...

ELSA: Time for your medication.

WALLY: I have my medication.

ELSA: Remember last time, Wally? Those palpitations and that fruit cocktail all down your shirt-front?

WALLY: Elsa—

ELSA: I'm sure Mr. Chaykin will excuse you. He's awfully accommodating.

(She exits.)

WALLY: Now you know how I came up with *Zeena the Jungle Queen*. Excuse me, Jules ...

(He exits.)

JULES: Good lord ...

(JULES, now surrounded by dolls, and ANGELA sit in silence for a moment.)

ANGELA: My dollies are going to eat you now.

(The lights come down. End of Act One.)

Act Two

(The act opens with a vision of the BLACK ANGEL, wings unfurling, talons reaching out. Then:

The living room. A bit of time has passed; JULES sits with ANGELA, who is admiring a small plate, white with a gold edge. ELSA is brushing ANGELA's hair.)

ANGELA: The gold around the edge is the same as the dot at the centre.

(She drops the plate, breaking it. JULES goes to help.)

Don't. We'll leave it there. Time will tell. Pink clouds.

ELSA: Soon.

ANGELA: Time is the passing shadow of nothing. So much fear there's no fear at all. The endless abnormal. Do you like my hair? Doll's hair. This dolly has the hair of a murderess. Ligeia Dexter Ward. She snatched a child from his bed, plunged her long nails into his soft breast, and flung him off a bridge in Paris. She was guillotined.

JULES: Does ... your dolly ... have a name?

ANGELA: Oh, no, I can't name them. Time will tell. Time is the decaying angel. It's a face that isn't there. I wonder when you'll die.

ELSA: You must be getting sleepy, Angela.

ANGELA: You're trying to poison me! There's poison in the tips of the brush!

ELSA: Don't be silly.

ANGELA: It's true!

ELSA: What about yesterday when you said I'd filled the bathtub with acid?

ANGELA: And look—today I'm all burned, my skin is all charred and black! Look! Do you see how hideous I am?

ELSA: Angela, you're as white as toothpaste.

ANGELA: Yes, Pepsodent. I'm the Pepsodent heiress.

ELSA: I spend half my time trying to get her off-topic.

JULES: You know, I think I should go.

ELSA: Oh?

JULES: I've really botched this—and after showing up at his door uninvited—

ELSA: Listen, that's how he wants you to feel.

JULES: I know, but ... it's uncomfortable. I can stay the night in Indian Springs.

ELSA: But you can't get there.

JULES: I'll call a cab.

ELSA: *(Laughing.)* A cab? Out here? On bomb night?

ANGELA: *(Touching JULES' arm.)* I was kidnapped. They made a hole in my brain.

ELSA: She really likes you.

JULES: Oh—thanks—she's very nice ... you're very nice.

ANGELA: I'm the little girl who trod on a loaf.

ELSA: The days must seem endless for her. You know, she used to love to read ...

JULES: You're doing this on purpose.

ELSA: Just being practical. She does like the company.

JULES: You really care for her well.

ELSA: Oh, we get along in our way.

(ELSA hands ANGELA another plate.)

ANGELA: *(Pleased.)* Heads up!

JULES: And Mr. Wolverton?

ELSA: Oh, I love it when you pry; you're so formal. Are you sure you want to know the terrible secrets of Hill House?

JULES: Sure. What goes on here?

ELSA: Oh, you make me feel all ... sphinxy. That's it! I'm the evil nurse in a scary story! What will you do with me?

JULES: Your victims rise from the morgue and kill you with syringes through your eyeballs.

ELSA: You really are creepy. But that wouldn't kill me.

JULES: Then—then they'll dissect you and leave your head in a bedpan, I don't know.

ELSA: Now you're insulted. I'm sorry, I didn't realize I was obliged to tell you everything.

JULES: Oh, not obliged. I mean, I've got eyes, I can figure it out.

ELSA: Listen to you. No, baby, sorry—you don't know scary like I do.

JULES: So tell me.

ELSA: You've a bit of drool there. Anyway, Angela's right here.

JULES: So? She's helpless.

ELSA: So you think.

(ANGELA breaks the plate.)

ANGELA: I'll tell! I'll tell everyone!

JULES: Right, she's Lucretia Borgia on a rolling throne.

ELSA: You think it's funny? Or can't you wrap your head around it. What did he tell you about her anyway?

JULES: Nothing—it's just general office knowledge ...

ELSA: What is?

JULES: His wife had a stroke.

ELSA: Oh. A stroke.

(Pause.)

JULES: What was it really?

ELSA: Why do you put so much trust in me?

JULES: You're her nurse.

ELSA: No—that's the funny thing, I came here long before Angela needed anyone's help. In fact she hired me to regulate Mr. Wolverton's ... dependencies. A well-financed tragedy, that's Wally.

JULES: So you count out the barbs and bennies, is that it?

ELSA: And water his scotch, as much as that helps—not much. I was her surrogate, in a way. Things were unravelling. He'd been ... pretty mean to her. Finally, she packed a bag and took a walk. He ran her down in his Oldsmobile.

JULES: You're joking.

ELSA: Of course, he said he couldn't see—it was night and his eyes were red enough to bleed. He even cried, right there on the road. But she knows the truth.

JULES: And how do you know?

ELSA: I was in the passenger seat.

JULES: Oh my god ...

ELSA: He insisted we go look for her, bring her back home. He shouldn't have been driving. When I saw her, I shouted at him, but—let's say his foot was slow on the brake despite the amphetamines in his brain. But she had time to turn around; I saw their eyes meet. She flew about ten feet, like a rag doll, staring back at us the whole time. She didn't even look surprised.

(Pause.)

JULES: I think I might have another drink.

ELSA: Certainly.

JULES: Why do you stay?

ELSA: Where would I go? It's the edge of the big nothing out here. I burned some bridges and forgot how to swim. Maybe I've hit the point when it seems normal to think that nothing will ever be normal again. And I've got her to think of, too.

JULES: Take her with you.

ELSA: Oh, you've got real trash novel instincts, don't you—fugitive nurse pushing her crippled charge across the endless desert in a wheelchair.

JULES: I'm serious.

ELSA: Listen, some of us, we're better off living in hell than in heaven. It just works out that way. But maybe now things can work out for you.

JULES: What do you mean?

ANGELA: Secret thing.

ELSA: Well, now you know something, don't you?

ANGELA: Listen ...

JULES: Oh ... you think I should use this to ...

ANGELA: It's—it's coming ...

ELSA: It's up to you.

ANGELA: Creeping up ...

ELSA: Dweller in the Tomb, dangling lives on a thread. Who would you hurt to change the world—and would it change?

ANGELA: It's coming—it's here—it's—it's—

(WALLY enters, stumbling.)

WALLY: Jeez, I broke my goddamn toe.

JULES: *(Unnerved.)* Wally—

WALLY: *(At the bar.)* Julie, I've had a vision. Floating on the bed like a dingy on the sea, and ... a vision. Bouncin' Bonnie Bunny, shipwrecked on the Island of the Lost Republicans.

JULES: Great.

WALLY: You tell me that's not horror? Hell, it's scarier than free jazz.

ELSA: Not as scary as some of things Mr. Chaykin knows.

JULES: I don't—lost Republicans—really scary.

ELSA: I'm sure.

WALLY: What are you up to, Elsa? *(To ANGELA.)* And you, you bug-eyed white witch, staring ... They haunt me, these two. Do you believe—listen now, Julie, do you believe two people can be one?

JULES: What? What do I say—sure, it happened to me once in a public washroom in Union Square? What are you asking me?

WALLY: These two. Sometimes I wake up at night ... one of them is at the foot of the bed, watching me ... Sometimes Elsa, sometimes my wife ... sometimes I can't tell ... Medusa one or Medusa two. Two halves of ... something. You know?

ELSA: He knows.

WALLY: I'm asking Jules—

ELSA: He knows, Wally.

JULES: No— *(Slight pause.)* Yes. I know.

WALLY: Good. *(Pause.)* Knows what?

JULES: About ... the thing.
WALLY: *(At a loss.)* Maybe I should sit down.
ELSA: I'm afraid Angela got on about your expert driving.
JULES: Oh God—
WALLY: You damn bitch—
ELSA: It was Angela who—
WALLY: Don't you dare—
> *(ANGELA breaks a plate.)*

ANGELA: Glass crunch flying. Flying. Then ink on my eyes, all black, black.
> *(Pause.)*

WALLY: Yes ... well ... it was an accident of course.
JULES: Then why call it a stroke? Why the need to lie?
WALLY: What could you possibly hope— *(Pause.)* You really do have a twisted devil crooked up inside you. Is it money you want?
JULES: No. *(Opening the portfolio.)* I want this story in *Scallywag*. Full-colour. Glossy stock. And the mind of every horny shaygets to set foot in a drugstore. That's what I want.
WALLY: You're obsessed.
JULES: Right, so you know I'm sincere. I want what I want, Wally.
WALLY: You just want to disgust me.
JULES: Oh, I don't have to disgust you. Maybe I can seduce you. Expose you. Maybe I can take you down, deep down into my bloody chamber, the horrid little room in my horrid little soul where I keep the things you don't want to see, all the dank, juicy things you think it's forbidden to look at.
ANGELA: And chocolate fudge soaking through the bandages.
JULES: Here—it's just the pencils so far, no inks, so it's still a bit—well, flexible ...
ELSA: *(Enthused.)* Looks creepy. Who's this?
> *(A transition begins. Music plays, Beethoven's "Coriolan" Overture, Opus Sixty-two.)*

JULES: Dare you ask? This is von Orlok.
ELSA: Orlok?

JULES: The Baron von Orlok ... the thoroughly, utterly de-nazified Baron Otto von Orlok. What did Otto do in the war? Depends on who's asking. Let's just say he's someone with the right connections to really make a killing—on the black market, that is. The year is 1948, we are somewhere in Germany, deep in the Black Forest, as a wedding party at Schloss Orlok spills into the night and two lovers escape to their own secret "Chamber of Souls ..."

(A fleeting vision of the BLACK ANGEL as the scene changes. Somewhere in Germany, 1948. The Baron's bedchamber in Schloss Orlok. We hear music and happy voices, off stage. Thunder. BARON OTTO VON ORLOK appears suddenly in a flash of lightning, carrying SYBILLE in his arms. They are formally dressed and wearing masks: Sybille's suggests the face of a doll, and Otto's, a dark and lushly feathered bird of prey. He carries her to the silk-draped bed.)

OTTO: At last ... the unmasking of the bride.

SYBILLE: And the groom.

OTTO: No. Let me stay a bird of prey, just for a moment. And let me admire my feast. *(He unmasks her.)*

SYBILLE: *(Embarrassed by his stare.)* Why a masked ball for a wedding party?

OTTO: Because love is just another mask. Were you unhappy? All I can give you is a black-market wedding, Sybille. Turnips into butter, butter into gold, and gold into you, my love, body and soul.

(SYBILLE turns from his touch. OTTO removes his mask.)

What have I said?

SYBILLE: Butter, beer and the good Yankee buck—is there a woman left in Germany who hasn't been told her worth?

OTTO: My God, is this Lily of Hell I've married?

SYBILLE: I thought—I hoped—you'd put the ring on my finger, one world would end and another world would—

OTTO: It did, Sybille.

(A last flash of lightning and roll of thunder. The scene changes. The bedchamber, the next morning. ZAZA, the extremely serious housekeeper, is serving SYBILLE coffee.)

SYBILLE: My new home ... so strange and grey. Oh, Zaza, I asked for tea.

ZAZA: Oh. My mistake. The first baroness preferred coffee.

SYBILLE: Nevermind then. But tomorrow ...

ZAZA: Of course. I see you've gathered some hyacinthe.

SYBILLE: Aren't they lovely?

ZAZA: In their way. The second baroness used to fill this room with Tibetan orchids.

SYBILLE: I only went as far as the garden. Tibet seemed extravagant.

ZAZA: I'll bring you some from the conservatory, it's much closer. *(She spills cream on SYBILLE.)* Oh—I'm so sorry—

SYBILLE: Oh, Zaza ... and Otto is sending someone to meet me ... Quick—I saw a kimono in the wardrobe—

ZAZA: That belonged to the first baroness ...

SYBILLE: I'm already drinking her coffee. Quick ...

(ZAZA fetches the kimono.)

ZAZA: Her perfection seemed almost oriental when she wore this.

SYBILLE: You're all so prone to elegies here.

ZAZA: There's been a lot of death here. May I ask who your visitor is?

SYBILLE: Oh, some artist Otto likes ...

ZAZA: Rotwang.

SYBILLE: Yes, that's it. I remember it sounded like something fungal.

ZAZA: He is a brilliant artist, a genius. Asta and Zenobia both sat for portraits.

(ROTWANG has entered, unseen. His clothes are dark, somber, almost medieval in their austerity; his left hand is artificial and gloved in glistening black.)

SYBILLE: Hmp. And how will he depict me—in some wholesome Germanic genre, bare-breasted with an armload of wheat?

ROTWANG: Or as Pandora opening the box of vice. How dare you—National Socialist painting was a useful experiment, nothing more. You've never even seen my work.

SYBILLE: Oh—I'm sorry—

ROTWANG: No—oh God, forgive me. That was inexcusable.

(A nervous silence.)

SYBILLE: Zaza, fresh coffee.

ZAZA: But—

SYBILLE: *(Dumping the hyacinthe.)* And wouldn't orchids be delightful?

(ZAZA exits.)

Are you Rotwang?

ROTWANG: I am.

(He takes her hand in his false hand, lifts it to his lips.)

Ah. I see you've lived through dark days.

SYBILLE: What?

ROTWANG: It's written on you. You're nothing like the other wives. You've had a taste of blood, haven't you?

SYBILLE: I—

ROTWANG: Yes, you'll be an exquisite subject for my work.

(The scene changes to Rotwang's studio, the next day. SYBILLE reclines on a black chaise, naked, the long crimson kimono draped about her. ROTWANG is sketching.)

SYBILLE: You do more looking than drawing.

ROTWANG: The other wives did not complain.

SYBILLE: And where are they now?

ROTWANG: Gone.

SYBILLE: How?

ROTWANG: You mustn't ask.

SYBILLE: I'm curious.

ROTWANG: That's the worst thing you could be.

SYBILLE: But—

ROTWANG: Please, Baroness—remember, silence is the language that God speaks.

SYBILLE: Yes, especially when he visits Germany. Though you can't blame him. We've all changed our language, haven't we— we call ourselves such different things. Not the shepherd but the sheep, not architect but artisan ... and an artist with a mechanical hand.

ROTWANG: I made this! I have reinvented my own body! What man today visits the extremes of his abilities?

SYBILLE: I would think we've all seen enough extremes.

ROTWANG: Yes, of course—my interest is the human body, but I've spilled more ink than blood, I assure you.

SYBILLE: So you are artist, scientist and mortician in one?

ROTWANG: Please, you must be the only German left with the stomach for questions.

SYBILLE: Questions fill me up. I'm a curious woman in a curious place—and I'm sure my curiosity is matched by the Baron's.

ROTWANG: But I am the Baron's curiosity. I sprang from his skull like the progeny of Jove.

SYBILLE: That's a peculiar relationship.

ROTWANG: I am his eyes.

SYBILLE: His eyes in the dark.

ROTWANG: Yes, exactly. I'll be your eyes too, if you'd like. Unless you're afraid to look.

(The scene changes: OTTO and SYBILLE, on the floor in the bedchamber. SYBILLE wears the doll-mask; OTTO holds a strap around her neck. ROTWANG secretly watches.)

OTTO: Sweet flesh.

SYBILLE: Otto—

OTTO: Sacred whore.

SYBILLE: Stop—

OTTO: Tell me you like this.

SYBILLE: No, I don't, I'm scared—

OTTO: Liar. Tell me you're my Lily of Hell.

SYBILLE: Yes.

OTTO: And anything I ask ...

SYBILLE: No—stop—

(She breaks free of OTTO and throws down the mask.)

You're scaring me.

OTTO: And here I thought you'd lost all fear.

SYBILLE: Does that make me no more than—

ROTWANG: *(Entering with tray of cold meat.)* A bit of cold lamb?

SYBILLE: Rotwang! You were—

ROTWANG: Was I?

SYBILLE: There are too many eyes here.

(She exits.)

OTTO: What is it, Rotwang—another grim forecast of Gotterdammerung?

ROTWANG: No, Baron. A vision. A dream from the future.

(The light changes as ROTWANG slips into a dream reality. The BLACK ANGEL appears behind him, embracing him, breathing into his ear.)

I see a shining shadow of a man, diamond-eyed, skin like black oil.

BLACK ANGEL: Beast.

ROTWANG: He has his fingers in me, hydra heaving carnivorous heads, reaching into me, exploding ...

BLACK ANGEL: Other.

ROTWANG: ... now coiled in a ball in my gut ... uncurling up my spine like a musky orchid, hands gripping my ribcage rung by rung, he blooms into my skull like a mushroom and he looks through my eyes. He is here, where I am ...

BLACK ANGEL: Pure.

ROTWANG: ... black is seeping through my skin, and I am fading into shadow ...

BLACK ANGEL: Pure.

(The BLACK ANGEL vanishes as the scene returns to the bedchamber. SYBILLE reappears, eavesdropping.)

ROTWANG: Africa is written on the map of my body.

OTTO: *(Gobbling up the lamb.)* At last! Our great work begins.

ROTWANG: But you realize my precious virus still lacks one vital component—the seed of life.

SYBILLE: A seed?

OTTO: You'll have what you need. Still, I didn't expect to abandon her to you so soon.

ROTWANG: Sybille will turn the key to her fate with her own hand. It is her nature.

SYBILLE: Fate ...

ROTWANG: Or perhaps she'll surprise you.

OTTO: None of my wives have yet surprized me. A sad thing, too.

(OTTO and ROTWANG exit.)

SYBILLE: Could it be? I'll be the first of three to bear a child ... into this House of the Dead. What dreams he'll have, what secrets whispered in his ear as he sleeps.

(Lights down. In the darkness, a scream. SYBILLE calls out.)

SYBILLE: Otto? Otto?

(ZAZA enters the bedchamber with a candelabrum. Thunder and lightning.)

ZAZA: Something is wrong?

SYBILLE: Where is Otto?

ZAZA: The Baron is often restless at night.

SYBILLE: I have to see him—I must—

ZAZA: But this is why I'm here. Why don't you tell me what's wrong? Did you ... see something?

SYBILLE: What do you mean?

ZAZA: *(Intimate.)* It's said the secrets of the schloss reveal themselves in the night ... in the dark ... Secrets within secrets. Sometimes ... some vague fear ... will seem to take shape ...

SYBILLE: Yes ... it—it could be ...

ZAZA: Tell me.

(The BLACK ANGEL appears in a flash of lightning as SYBILLE speaks.)

SYBILLE: I dreamt—I thought I dreamt someone—something—in the dark ...

BLACK ANGEL: Come to me.

(The BLACK ANGEL disappears.)

ZAZA: My god. The angel of death.

SYBILLE: Or of love.

ZAZA: Ah. Meaning the Baron ...?

SYBILLE: When—when I'm with him—I'm sorry, I shouldn't—

ZAZA: But you want to tell someone. Don't you?

(Thunder and lightning.)

SYBILLE: When he closes in on me like a tender wolf ... One touch, and I'm lost, I feel a dark hunger rushing into me ... He fills me with his savage fire, and then ...

ZAZA: Then a child.

SYBILLE: And where are Asta and Zenobia's children? My husband seems satisfied with just the bride.

ZAZA: You should try to sleep.

SYBILLE: Why do I love him even though I know he's ... oh God ...

ZAZA: The second baroness found a hot buttermilk brought a sleep as deep as ... well, very deep.

SYBILLE: And the first?

ZAZA: Vaishnavite yoga. She hung from the chandelier like a drowsy moth, in a world beyond our own. Perhaps you'd like the buttermilk.

SYBILLE: Oh, I'm burning, burning ...

(A crash of thunder and lightning as OTTO enters. SYBILLE lets out a startled cry.)

OTTO: Well, what's this happy little scene?

SYBILLE: Otto—you're dressed?

ZAZA: I'll bring the buttermilk ...

(She exits.)

SYBILLE: Otto—?

OTTO: I have a plane waiting. I'm expected in Dakar by dawn.

SYBILLE: Dakar? In Africa?

OTTO: Unless they've misplaced it. The Americans have contracted my ships, we're to transport small pox vaccine.

SYBILLE: But it hasn't even been a week—

OTTO: We have weeks and years ahead, I promise you. 'Til then, a gift ... *(He produces an iron ring thick with keys.)* Keys to every room, to the kitchen and the cockloft, keys to doors that haven't been opened since the darkest days ... You are mistress of the labyrinth now. *(Hesitates over a key.)* Only—

SYBILLE: *(Eager.)* What's that? The key to your heart?

OTTO: No. To my hell. A dull, dusty little room in the east tower. I go there ... to sort through my little tragedies. You wouldn't like it ... full of spiders. But you must promise me one thing, Sybille; promise me you'll use every key on the ring but this, and allow me a silent place. Promise me.

SYBILLE: I promise.

OTTO: Come. It's the dead of night.

(The scene changes. The next day, near dusk. SYBILLE is in the bedchamber.)

SYBILLE: So it's a game of death he wants, and not a child ...

(The BLACK ANGEL appears.)

BLACK ANGEL: Come to me.

SYBILLE: *(Producing the key.)* Yes, this has to be a way to see ...

BLACK ANGEL: You must.

SYBILLE: No, I don't dare ...

BLACK ANGEL: Look.

(He disappears.)

SYBILLE: My fears and my dreams—they've become the same. How did this happen? And how to be the tiger, and not tiger-food ...

(CONNIE enters, a meat cleaver in one hand. She silently crosses to SYBILLE.)

Zaza—? You're not—no—stay back—

(CONNIE gently touches SYBILLE's cheek.)

Who are you? Why do you ... look so sad?

(CONNIE beckons her to follow.)

Yes, I'll follow you. Show me the secrets.

(CONNIE leads SYBILLE through corridors of shadow and light.

SYBILLE recites.)

Past dark past fear
Pandora passe-partout
through the labyrinth
through the mirror
to shadowland

(The BLACK ANGEL becomes the door to the forbidden chamber. He lets SYBILLE pass, then captures CONNIE in a vampiric embrace. They disappear. The scenes becomes the forbidden chamber: an operating room, flashes of gleaming, antiseptic chrome. On a trolley, bizarre surgical instruments and a rack of hypodermic needles. An operating table. Overhead, a large surveillance eye, literally ocular in design. Arcane graffiti, algebraic runes marked in chalk on the walls.

SYBILLE enters, singing to herself.)

"That's a problem for tomorrow,
I don't need to borrow sorrow,
T'morrow's nothing, to be blunt,
You can shove it where you want ..."

(She sees the surgical instruments.)

What are these? Vicious snippers ...

(The surveillance eye casts a flickering beam of light on her. A flutter of wings.)

What's that? Wings—

(An owl hoots.)

Stupid owls. Stupid—

(The BLACK ANGEL appears out of the darkness behind her, the shadows of its wings stretching to a great height, and seizes her. Blackout.

There is music. When the lights return, SYBILLE's hands are bound by chains above her head. ROTWANG is with her as she regains consciousness.)

ROTWANG: Do you like this music? Metamorphosen. Richard Strauss wrote it as a lament for the destruction of German culture.

SYBILLE: Rotwang ...

ROTWANG: Welcome to Valhalla. One of its darker corners.

SYBILLE: It's you—you led me—

ROTWANG: You came. Only a fool could resist, and the Baron has yet to marry a fool. He prefers the unfortunate, the tragic.

SYBILLE: Where in hell—

ROTWANG: Hell on earth. Death's workshop.

SYBILLE: And you its mechanic.

ROTWANG: Yes, Sybille, I am the spider in the cerebrum; I am the Baron's curiosity and here I seek my satisfaction.

SYBILLE: Among the dead.

ROTWANG: They are excellent company. Full of secrets that yield to the touch of a blade.

SYBILLE: Otto—

ROTWANG: —is in Africa.

SYBILLE: Why? *(Pause.)* The small pox vaccine ...

ROTWANG: Oh, excellent. You're very good at this. The vaccine has a poisonous little friend travelling along ...

SYBILLE: But why—?

(A vision of a woman briefly appears, draped in red and bathed in red light, wearing the doll's-face mask, eyes and hands lifted toward heaven.)

ROTWANG: Oh, it's part of an experiment, a very valuable experiment we've been planning ever since Asta fell victim to a strange burning rash, creeping like a giant red spider through her skin ... What a fascinating discovery that was.

SYBILLE: Of what?

ROTWANG: Of a disease, of course.

(Another vision: a woman, also masked and draped in shimmering silver.)

Zenobia complex is my own name for it—you see, it was when Zenobia withered like a wraith that I knew I had created the most perfect disease in the world, the black seed of a viral cleansing.

SYBILLE: A seed—you do want my child ...

ROTWANG: No no no, I don't need the whole child. Just the simple spark of life—it will be the very engine of my disease.

SYBILLE: You're the disease.

ROTWANG: Oh, brave words—and so many at hand. When I slice you open, will brave words slither out?

SYBILLE: Rotwang—if you have any human kindness—

ROTWANG: I'm afraid not. Any emotion for me is a prison.

SYBILLE: You monster—

ROTWANG: Yes ... I'm always looking, you see; looking has made me a monster.

SYBILLE: And dear Otto is your pimp.

ROTWANG: Ah, you have it all worked out, don't you? The Baron truly does marry his equal in curiosity. But oh, how the first two fretted over that key. You're the quickest to your doom by being the boldest. *(Caressing her with a scapel.)* Perhaps because you understand ... death is the lover you cannot tear your eyes from.

SYBILLE: *(Trying to conceal her genuine arousal.)* You're—you're mad—

ROTWANG: Mad, you say? Is it mad to know the universe is an endless apocalypse, its only harmony the harmony of death? Is it mad that the future is rushing to meet me?

SYBILLE: No one will follow a fascist now.

ROTWANG: The heart is a fascist, and yet we follow it. And in my black heart, you are the Queen of Hell.

SYBILLE: Oh lord ...

ROTWANG: You are ... *excited?*

SYBILLE: No ...

ROTWANG: It will be my gift to you, Sybille—the life only an artist can give. Does it matter if my medium is death?

SYBILLE: But my gifts, Rotwang—my gifts are sweeter.

ROTWANG: What?

SYBILLE: I'll give you anything you want ... if you cut out the fetus and let me go.

ROTWANG: *(Taken aback.)* My God—

SYBILLE: Come to me, Rotwang. Burn with me.

ROTWANG: In a flame like ice? You surprise me, Sybille.

SYBILLE: Anything you want ...

ROTWANG: And what would I want with a Berlin whore, when I have an agent of the night, a black angel to serve my black whims.

(The BLACK ANGEL appears.)

SYBILLE: Good lord!

(The laughing ANGEL wraps itself around ROTWANG.)

ROTWANG: Here the boundaries of the real disappear, like the shedding of skin.

(He unmasks the ANGEL. It is ZAZA, harlequin-black around her eyes, like a second mask.)

SYBILLE: Zaza!

ZAZA: Yes, me—I'm your nightmare!

SYBILLE: But why—

ZAZA: To make you look, of course. To turn your lust to fear. Are you not horrified?

SYBILLE: Zaza, you look ridiculous.

ZAZA: I am pure! Reborn in the hands of this beautiful man, my black angel, who takes me to the borderlands, where I scarcely know myself.

ROTWANG: Zaza is such enormous fun. She'll do anything.

SYBILLE: And what do you do to her?

ROTWANG: Many things.

ZAZA: Dark and wonderful things. He has given me the greatest gift of all. He has given me ... a penis!

(ZAZA reveals a large, fleshy phallus.)

ROTWANG: Well, a working model.

(SYBILLE laughs.)

(Enraged.) How dare you? This is the flesh of the future—why aren't you horrified? How can you laugh in the face of the unravelling?

SYBILLE: It's not her face that strikes me as funny.

ROTWANG: Stop it! Where is your fear?

ZAZA: Beauty thinks she's fierce enough to play with the beast.

ROTWANG: Well, she hasn't seen your invulnerable viscera.

ZAZA: Yes, show her! We'll show her!

ROTWANG: Zaza is a catalogue of kinks, I'm afraid. She especially enjoys needles. Don't you, Zaza?

ZAZA: Oh, yes ...

SYBILLE: Indeed.

(The music returns as ZAZA reclines on the operating table, under chiarioscuro surgical lighting.)

ROTWANG: *(Injecting her.)* A little visit with Morpheus today ... Breath deep ...

ZAZA: Red kisses, deep red ...

ROTWANG: To be so free, to know that the soul is the prison of the body, and that the body can escape through its own mutability.

(ROTWANG begins to operate. The BLACK ANGEL appears, embracing and caressing SYBILLE.)

You wish to share my feast of fierce delights? Then look: ecstasy and death ...

BLACK ANGEL: Universe.

ROTWANG: ... our gods and our monsters ...

BLACK ANGEL: Endless.

ROTWANG: ... they exist here, under the skin ...

BLACK ANGEL: Apocalypse.

ROTWANG: ... waiting to be reborn ... You don't believe me, but I'll show you—Yes! I'll show you all!

(Blood spurts up. The BLACK ANGEL disappears.)

Oops— *(Pause.)* Oh. *(Pause.)* Well, that did it.

SYBILLE: You've killed her?

ROTWANG: She twitched! It's her fault, she's ruined all my brilliant work. Still, she's very beautiful this way ...

SYBILLE: Dead. Dead.

(As ROTWANG lingers over ZAZA, the BLACK ANGEL reappears and frees SYBILLE from her bonds.)

ROTWANG: My volcanic enigma ...

BLACK ANGEL: Beast.

ROTWANG: ... face like a mask ...

BLACK ANGEL: Other.

ROTWANG: ... as if the horrors she'd seen ...

BLACK ANGEL: Pure.

SYBILLE: Oh, yes ...

ROTWANG: ... had washed it clean.

SYBILLE: Yes ...

(The BLACK ANGEL disappears. SYBILLE is free.)

ROTWANG: Poor, stupid Zaza ...

SYBILLE: No more stupid than you.

ROTWANG: Sybille! No—how could—you can't escape here. There is nowhere you can run, nowhere you can hide.

SYBILLE: I don't want to run, I want to see.

ROTWANG: What?

SYBILLE: Show me more. Open her up—let's see this poisonous garden you've grown.

ROTWANG: No—stay back—

SYBILLE: *(Clutching a hypodermic needle.)* Show me more!

ROTWANG: My god, what's happened to you? What demon has awakened inside—

(Unseen by SYBILLE and ROTWANG, ZAZA has roused.)

ZAZA: Rotwang! You bastard ...

ROTWANG: Zaza!

ZAZA: What are you doing with her? You said it was my uterus you loved!

ROTWANG: How could she even be conscious?

ZAZA: You promised me barbed labia! Steel fallopia!

ROTWANG: *(Grabs the empty hypodermic needle.)* Oh no! It's not anaesthetic—it's schizophrenic brain fluid!

ZAZA: *(Closing on him.)* I told you not to eat that strudel but you just wouldn't listen! Why didn't you listen?

(SYBILLE stabs ZAZA.)

Ack! Sauerbraten!

(SYBILLE laughs triumphantly as ZAZA falls at her feet.)

ROTWANG: Good lord!

SYBILLE: There! I've sent an angel to hell! Look at her twitch!

ROTWANG: Stop—

SYBILLE: Oh, it's fantastic!

ROTWANG: You are a demon ...

SYBILLE: I'm as human as you, Rotwang. That's why you love me so.

ROTWANG: No—it was your fear I loved.

SYBILLE: *(Closing on him, seductive and malevolent.)* Oh, but you've taken me so much deeper than fear, my sweet ...

ROTWANG: The blood on you—I can't bear it!
(ZAZA has again revived.)
ZAZA: Rotwang—darling—
ROTWANG: Damn! Get away!
ZAZA: *(Rising.)* You were my world! My cosmos!
ROTWANG: Don't make me kill you again!
(ZAZA plunges the hypodermic needle into his neck.)
ZAZA: I don't love you anymore!
SYBILLE: Yes! Kill him!
ROTWANG: Oh, shit—
SYBILLE: Kill him!
(ROTWANG looks at the needle.)
ROTWANG: You idiot! The typhus concentrate—deadlier than the black mamba! I can't die like this! My work—my life's work—I still have so much to—No! Time cannot silence me! It cannot— *(He collapses abruptly.)* This is bad.
SYBILLE: Die, monster ...
ROTWANG: Sybille—how can you—I love you—
SYBILLE: Die, damn you ...
ROTWANG: My inspiration ... the joy your pain would have brought me ... but no ... only silence ...
(He dies.)
ZAZA: Oh god, I must look like hell.
(ZAZA dies. SYBILLE laughs maniacally. Lights suggest a passage of time. When she speaks again, she has gone mad.)
SYBILLE: *(Singing.)* "That's a problem for tomorrow,
I don't need to borrow sorrow,
T'morrow's nothing, to be blunt ... you can shove ... it ..."
(OTTO enters.)
OTTO: Hello. Thought I'd drop in, since the door was unlocked.
(SYBILLE reclines on the operating table, anxious with desire.)
SYBILLE: Ah ... Love's black angel.
OTTO: Well, look at Rotwang. I thought he might be too much a thing of shadow to ever shed a drop of blood. Ah well ... I'll have

to find myself another evil genius to play with. And poor Zaza. She looks like hell.

SYBILLE: Oh my love ... come ... I'm burning ...

OTTO: *(Gently.)* And your innocence is all but ash.

SYBILLE: My love, your eyes are dead.

OTTO: As dead as my wives. But in death there is peace, isn't there?

SYBILLE: Pure love I give you, pure.

OTTO: No, my dove, not pure. You've learned the game too well. So I'll have your pretty head.

(He picks up the vicious snippers.)

SYBILLE: I'm your Lily of Hell ...

OTTO: Your head, my love.

SYBILLE: No, not my head! Not my—

(OTTO snips. Blackout. A thud.

A shadowy vision of the BLACK ANGEL holding SYBILLE's head is seen while JULES' voice is heard, as the Dweller in the Tomb.)

JULES: Oops—heads up! Looks like Sybille lost her noggin over love—how sweet! I guess you could call it a triumph of the swill for Otto—and with him still on the loose, the blutwurst is yet to come! Heh heh heh ... I'll save that vile yelp-yarn for our next tête-a-tête-less. Time to close the Tomb of Doom—but don't fret! I'll be sending you Otto for a viscid visit, and he'll put more than a chill in your blood ... Don't bother locking your door! Heh heh heh ...

(The scene has returned to the living room.)

So there it is.

ANGELA: Glowing spiders.

WALLY: This is what you want?

ANGELA: Webs ...

JULES: It's what I want, Wally.

ANGELA: ... like diamond threads.

WALLY: Do you have any idea how humiliating—

JULES: Shut up, Wally—I'm sick of you getting a pole up your ass every time there's a tough decision.

ELSA: My god, I've created a monster.

WALLY: What, you think Joe McCarthy's planted one of his zombie electrodes in my pineal gland?

ANGELA: I'm the beauty zombie! I'm the blood-splattered prom queen!

WALLY: You think I'm so spineless I'd let myself be blackmailed by a corpse-humping crypto-Nazi bootboy—

JULES: Hey—

WALLY: It's right here—

JULES: That's just a character—

WALLY: You can go to hell, Jules.

JULES: Show me the way, Wally.

ELSA: Maybe we should let the boys hash this out themselves, Angela.

ANGELA: Where are the big lights?

ELSA: Come on ...

ANGELA: I'm waiting for the big lights!

ELSA: Angela—

ANGELA: No!

ELSA: Fine! Vicious little monkey—you can stay here all night then!

(ELSA locks the wheels of Angela's wheelchair.)

ANGELA: What—what—good! Good, I like it here! I like it!

ELSA: I'll be in my room.

WALLY: Stay here.

ELSA: I said—

WALLY: No, stay here, Elsa. Listen to Julie here. For the sake of a bunch of gory doodles that would get you kicked out of a matchbook art school, he's going to take the knives to my life.

JULES: The facts speak for themselves.

WALLY: No, they need you. They need you coming at me with your vicious snippers and a crazy grin. Come on, let's see it. I'm not afraid of you. Not as afraid as you are of yourself. Too bad you don't know everything.

ELSA: He knows enough.

WALLY: Who ever does?

JULES: There—there can't be more ...

WALLY: What does he know? He knows amphetamines, speeding, Angela flying ... that's all. But not how peaceful I felt doing it, how I lined it up like a pool shot, how I wanted to kill her in front of her lover.

(Pause.)

ELSA: If that bomb doesn't go off soon, I think I just might explode from the tedium.

WALLY: Nobody's innocent in this house. That's what makes us a family. Come on, Julie, show me you're tough, show me what sort of monster's in you.

ANGELA: The thing from under the stairs.

ELSA: Hush.

WALLY: Phone the county sheriff. Tell him you're a queer commie from Greenwich Village nose-deep in hot dirt—let's see who he whips up his angry mob for—me or you, or maybe Elsa here, the she-wolf of Cell Block Lilith.

ELSA: What a pig you are.

WALLY: What other defense do I have? You'll do anything—you'll even coerce poor stupid Julie, who doesn't know a damn—

ELSA: I'll do anything? You ran her down!

WALLY: I saved her from you.

ANGELA: Black thing.

ELSA: Did she ask to be saved?

JULES: Please—I don't see—

ELSA: For Christ's sake, all I did was give her a novel by Colette.

WALLY: You changed her.

ELSA: She would have changed on her own.

ANGELA: Hungry thing.

WALLY: You're a deadly black poison, you. We had the desert sky and the deep night and miles of nothing but each other.

ELSA: You had a Dexamyl dependency, that's what you had.

ANGELA: The thing that breathes hate in my mouth!

ELSA: Angela—

WALLY: You think I'd ever let any harm come to her?

ELSA: That's right, Wally—you take real good care of all of us. That's why she always cries out in the night, not just scared, no—it's real pain.

ANGELA: The thing that tears me open!

ELSA: That's why somebody locks the door to her room so I can't get in. Isn't that right, Wally?

WALLY: You bloodsucking—

ANGELA: I should have died! I should have—

WALLY: Shut up or I'll smash this bloody doll's—

ANGELA: No! No!

ELSA: Stop it!

(They are grouped around ANGELA, ELSA ready to hit her, and WALLY brandishing a doll. They catch JULES' eye. Slight pause.)

WALLY: Another scotch?

JULES: I—I—

WALLY: Come on, we're playing spot the monster, Julie. Can you do it? You don't need goggles from Dimension X.

JULES: I—oh wow—

ELSA: What's wrong?

JULES: Nothing—

ELSA: You're all flushed ...

JULES: Please, I—

WALLY: Maybe you could give him something.

JULES: No—

ELSA: You look terrible.

JULES: It's okay—

ELSA: Here, this is a very mild sedative ...

JULES: No—it was—a mental image—just hit me—

ELSA: Listen, you're a mess.

JULES: One face inside another—look—I gotta go—

WALLY: It's too late, Jules—they'll have closed the roads. You're here for the night.

JULES: Oh God—I never knew—I never—where are those pills? Oh god ... what a horribly miserable existence you have.

WALLY: Thanks for pointing that out.

JULES: And I love it. Look at me—big bug-eyes, thinking pink, I'm thrilled to the tips of my HBs. What a stink you've got coming off you. And you know what? It's got me hard.

WALLY: And you say you won't do porn.

JULES: Ha! Maybe I will. I mean it, I like this—you've got me throbbing, you and your nasty ugly secrets. Spot the monster. How about me? Hey, give me a plate of somebody else's misery and a side of malaise and I'm grinning like a horny devil. After all, there's no freude like schadenfreude, right?

WALLY: Jules, what are you—

JULES: We're both idiots—you know that? I'm not assimilating Auschwitz—I'm making a goddamn meal of it! Oh, man ... This is it, Wally, this is the one thing we can never cure.

WALLY: What the hell are you talking about?

JULES: You want to hear scary? See, Wally, I lied about my mother ... about all that stuff meaning nothing to her. My mother did lose someone. Her sister Tosha. I don't know the details, all I know is Tosha died in the camps and it took at least four years for word to reach us.

My mother's reaction was to cook. No tears, no grief, just latkes, stacks and stacks of potato latkes, all day, half the night, then again, first thing in the morning, more latkes. My poor father, helpless man, he's hoisting latkes on all their neighbours, he's wrapping them up for the milkman ... Finally, after two days of this, she reaches the bottom of the potato sack, thank God. And we assume she's come to terms through her latkes.

Then, one in the morning, my father, he calls and says, "She's started making blintzes."

I grab a cab over. I walk into the kitchen and what do you know, it's Sadye's inferno. The walls are smeared with strawberry jam—I mean smeared, splattered, dripping, like an abattoir, I mean I'd never seen so much strawberry jam, it was horrific.

And there's my mother like a white demon, coated in flour like a giant knish, pounding the crap out of a block of cream cheese with a meat mallet.

I ask her what she's doing and suddenly she's perfectly calm, she puts down the mallet and I see her arm ...

It's all cut up ... clean but deep, really deep in the flesh. Three thoughts, like rockets—first, it's oh my God she's so crazy she doesn't realize she's hurt her—then no, look at where they are, she's been trying to—but they have shapes. Shapes like ... a four—the number four deliberately sliced ... and a seven. A one. Sort of a two.

ANGELA: I should have died.

JULES: She ... I ...

(He slaps ANGELA hard across the face.)

Oh God—I don't know why I—I just did, I was so full of hate. I hated her. I thought, how can you give in to this, give in to the dead, to the dead past. And then—then I felt what I was feeling. The hatred. From somewhere so deep inside me ...

ANGELA: Loving the dead.

WALLY: I'm sorry, Jules—I didn't realize—

JULES: Oh, I'm not through, Wally—I haven't even got to the scary part.

WALLY: Jules, you don't have to—

JULES: Sure I do. Me and my monsters, I never run out of them. I'm going to scare the living crap right out of you ...

ELSA: Maybe these aren't the mild sedatives ...

JULES: Do you know what I did? What I'd never done. I walked out, I turned and walked out without saying a word. I headed back downtown but when I got to my building I kept going. Through the streets. To the piers.

Why shouldn't I? I'm drawn, but more than that, it's like I'm blind and being led on a route of pure sense, a map of smell. Danger's perfume. I'm changing, shedding skin ... coarse hair, crackle of static, all on end. Eyes shooting red rays into a skeleton labyrinth, walls and beams and pipes. And men like passing shadows.

Why shouldn't I? Here in the dark, we become the same. All around me, sounds of pleasure, taken, given, shared. A secret released to hum in the air between us, now that we are all alike.

(A shadowy figure appears. It is the third incarnation of the BLACK ANGEL, bound, gagged and struggling.)

And there ... someone ... he's caught my scent, and his is good, too. Breathless. Silence. And then ...
hot breath
touch
breath
Why shouldn't—
the body escapes
the prison of the soul
Why sh—

(The BLACK ANGEL disapppears.)

Scared yet, Wally? It goes on—I did more than that, I did anyone who wanted it, all night, a feast of flesh, I was the wolf, the beast, hell I even drew blood, it was fantastic. Incredible. The most powerful I'd ever felt.

WALLY: You were upset, you were—

JULES: I was free. It was the last moment in my life I was free of the memory of her eyes—swollen, red, looking at me, into me, asking me to understand ... that frozen moment, when I couldn't tear my eyes off her pain.

ELSA: Well, it—it must be difficult—

JULES: You think so? I mean, hell, I did it. How could I be capable of—Shouldn't I feel ashamed? Horrified? Is this what happens?

ANGELA: All of us.

JULES: Is it?

ANGELA: All of us.

(JULES looks at the artwork.)

JULES: These are the answers I came up with. *(He rips the work in half.)* Wrong again.

ELSA: What are you doing?

WALLY: Jules—you don't have to—

JULES: You want silence, Wally? I'll give you the silence of monsters.

WALLY: You still might have found someone to publish—

JULES: Oh fuck off, Wally, they're all like you. And maybe I'm no better. You can stop looking at me like I'm going to smash your glass bungalow. No more scary stories.

WALLY: Yes. Let's call it a night, Jules.
(A flare gun goes off in the distance.)
WALLY: Hold on ...
ANGELA: Falling angel, down we go.
WALLY: The flare signal. This is it—come and watch, Jules.
ELSA: The air—do you feel the way the air has changed?
ANGELA: We're all praying for dawn.
ELSA: Do you want to watch from the patio, Angela?
ANGELA: Yes, yes, heads up!
WALLY: Come right back in this time. I don't want glowing wheelchair treads through here for weeks on end again.
(ELSA and ANGELA exit.)
The flash could come anytime.
JULES: Sure.
WALLY: Don't look so grim, Julie. Tomorrow's brighter than you think—always is. That's the one thing you can count on.
(Brilliant light floods into the room.)
ELSA: *(Off stage.)* There!
ANGELA: *(Off stage.)* Big light! Big light!
WALLY: Yes! Isn't it beautiful? Isn't it—
(Blackout, followed by a thundering roar. End of the play.)